ONES AND TWOS

by Marthe Jocelyn and Nell Jocelyn

Tundra Books

Published in Canada by Tundra Books,
75 Sherbourne Street, Toronto, Ontario M5A 2P9

Published in the United States by Tundra Books of Northern New York,
P.O. Box 1030, Plattsburgh, New York 12901

Library of Congress Control Number: 2010928787

Library and Archives Canada Cataloguing in Publication

Jocelyn, Marthe
Ones and twos / author: Marthe Jocelyn ; illustrator: Nell Jocelyn.

ISBN 978-1-77049-220-2

1. Counting--Juvenile literature. I. Jocelyn , Nell II. Title.

QA113.J633 2011   j513.2'11   C2010-903161-X

We acknowledge the financial support of the Government of Canada through the Book Publishing Industry Development Program (BPIDP) and that of the Government of Ontario through the Ontario Media Development Corporation's Ontario Book Initiative. We further acknowledge the support of the Canada Council for the Arts and the Ontario Arts Council for our publishing program.

ONTARIO ARTS COUNCIL
CONSEIL DES ARTS DE L'ONTARIO

Printed and bound in China

1 2 3 4 5 6   16 15 14 13 12 11

One bird, two eggs,

One girl, two legs.

One bench, two bags,

One pole, two flags.

One cloud, two kites,

One bun, two bites.

One crust,

two crumbs,

One lone,

two chums.

One swoops, two walk,

One sings, two talk.

 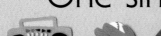   

Two wave,

one flies,

Two share

one prize.

One nest,

two heads.

Two girls,

one bed.